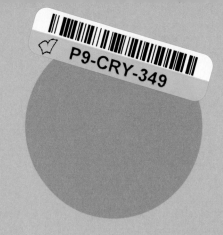

A Note to Parents and Caregivers:

Read-it! Readers are for children who are just starting on the amazing road to reading. These beautiful books support both the acquisition of reading skills and the love of books.

The PURPLE LEVEL presents basic topics and objects using high frequency words and simple language patterns.

The RED LEVEL presents familiar topics using common words and repeating sentence patterns.

The BLUE LEVEL presents new ideas using a larger vocabulary and varied sentence structure.

The YELLOW LEVEL presents more challenging ideas, a broad vocabulary, and wide variety in sentence structure.

The GREEN LEVEL presents more complex ideas, an extended vocabulary range, and expanded language structures.

The ORANGE LEVEL presents a wide range of ideas and concepts using challenging vocabulary and complex language structures.

When sharing a book with your child, read in short stretches, pausing often to talk about the pictures. Have your child turn the pages and point to the pictures and familiar words. And be sure to reread favorite stories or parts of stories.

There is no right or wrong way to share books with children. Find time to read with your child, and pass on the legacy of literacy.

Adria F. Klein, Ph.D.
Professor Emeritus
California State University
San Bernardino, California

To my dear friend, Katy. —S.A.Z.

Editor: Christianne C. Jones
Page Production: Amy Bailey Muehlenhardt
Creative Director: Keith Griffin
Editorial Director: Carol Jones
Managing Editor: Catherine Neitge
The illustrations in this book were created with watercolor.

Picture Window Books
5115 Excelsior Boulevard
Suite 232
Minneapolis, MN 55416
877-845-8392
www.picturewindowbooks.com

Printed in the United States of America.

Library of Congress Cataloging-in-Publication Data
Dahl, Michael.
The princess and the tower / by Michael Dahl ; illustrated by Svetlana Zhurkin.
p. cm. — (Read-it! readers)
Summary: A reader of fairy tales, a young princess longs for the day when a prince
will save her from a dragon or witch, but when she finally is chased and locked in a
tower she decides to take matters into her own hands.
ISBN 1-4048-1184-2 (hardcover)
[1. Self-reliance—Fiction. 2. Princesses—Fiction. 3. Witches—Fiction.
4. Dragons—Fiction. 5. Fairy tales.] I. Zhurkin, Svetlana, ill. II. Title. III. Series.

PZ8.D133Pri 2005
[E]—dc22
                                              2005003898

The Princess and the Tower

by Michael Dahl
illustrated by Svetlana A. Zhurkin

Special thanks to our advisers for their expertise:

Adria F. Klein, Ph.D.
Professor Emeritus, California State University
San Bernardino, California

Susan Kesselring, M.A.
Literacy Educator
Rosemount–Apple Valley–Eagan (Minnesota) School District

PICTURE WINDOW BOOKS
Minneapolis, Minnesota

Princess Lily liked reading fairy tales.

She read stories about dragons
and witches.

She read stories about brave princes.

6

And she read stories about princesses just like herself.

"Someday, a prince will save me from a terrible dragon and a scary witch," said Lily. "Then we will live happily ever after."

One day, Princess Lily was walking outside and reading. She heard a terrible roar. Lily looked behind her. She could not believe her eyes!

A witch and a dragon were running toward her.

Lily started to run. She ran toward a tall tower at the end of the path. The dragon and the witch were close behind her.

They chased Princess Lily right into the tower.

13

Lily ran up the stairs and into a room at the top of the tower. She quickly shut the door.

Then, Lily heard a click.

"Oh no! The witch has locked me in," cried Lily.

Lily cried and cried. "Maybe a prince will come rescue me," she said. "Just like in my fairy tale books. I will sit here and wait."

1000 DESSERT RECIPES

Cinderella's
Favorite Desserts

AKES

OOK

17

A week went by, and nothing happened.
Luckily, the room was filled with food
and cookbooks.

18

Lily learned how to make delicious desserts.

"I hope the prince likes chocolate cake," said Lily.

Two weeks went by, and a prince never came to rescue Princess Lily.

"This is silly," said Lily. "I'll just have to rescue myself."

So, Lily carefully climbed out
the window and down the
tall tower.

21

At the bottom of the tower, Lily
stopped. The witch was waiting
for her.

"Why didn't you use the stairs?"
asked the witch.

"You locked me inside," said Lily.

"I locked the door so the dragon would not eat you," said the witch. "The dragon was chasing both of us!"

25

"Then, I turned the dragon into a dragonfly," said the witch.

"I unlocked the door, but you were asleep.
I didn't want to wake you, so I left. I thought
you would see that the door was unlocked,"
the witch said.

"I didn't try the door when I woke up," said Lily. "I guess I was too busy waiting for someone to rescue me."

28

"Waiting for who?" asked the witch.

"Never mind," said Lily. "Do you like chocolate cake?"

"I sure do!" the witch said.

Princess Lily and the witch went back to the top of the tower. They ate cake and talked about all the books they had read—fairy tales, cookbooks, spell books, and more!

More *Read-it!* Readers

Bright pictures and fun stories help you practice your reading skills. Look for more books at your level.

Alex and Sarah by Gilles Tibo
Alex and the Team Jersey by Gilles Tibo
Alex and Toolie by Gilles Tibo
Clever Cat by Karen Wallace
Felicio's Incredible Invention by Mireille Villeneuve
Flora McQuack by Penny Dolan
Izzie's Idea by Jillian Powell
Mysteries for Felicio by Mireille Villeneuve
Naughty Nancy by Anne Cassidy
Parents Do the Weirdest Things! by Louise Tondreau-Levert
Peppy, Patch, and the Bath by Marisol Sarrazin
Peppy, Patch, and the Postman by Marisol Sarrazin
Peppy, Patch, and the Socks by Marisol Sarrazin
The Princess and the Frog by Margaret Nash
The Roly-Poly Rice Ball by Penny Dolan
Run! by Sue Ferraby
Sausages! by Anne Adeney
Stickers, Shells, and Snow Globes by Dana Meachen Rau
Theodore the Millipede by Carole Tremblay
The Truth About Hansel and Gretel by Karina Law
Willie the Whale by Joy Oades

Looking for a specific title or level? A complete list of *Read-it!* Readers is available on our Web site:
www.picturewindowbooks.com